Destiny
the Pop star
Fairy

To Emilia, with love

Special thanks
to Rachel Elliot

ORCHARD BOOKS
338 Euston Road, London NW1 3BH
Orchard Books Australia
Level 17/207 Kent Street, Sydney, NSW 2000
A Paperback Original

First published in 2009 by Orchard Books

HiT entertainment

A CIP catalogue record for this book is available
from the British Library.

ISBN 978 1 40830 473 0

1 3 5 7 9 10 8 6 4 2

Printed and bound in China by Imago

The paper and board used in this paperback are natural recyclable
products made from wood grown in sustainable forests. The
manufacturing processes conform to the environmental regulations
of the country of origin.

Orchard Books is a division of Hachette Children's Books,
an Hachette UK company

www.hachette.co.uk

Destiny
the Pop Star
Fairy

by Daisy Meadows

ORCHARD BOOKS

www.rainbowmagic.co.uk

The Fairyland Palace

Harwoods Department Store

The Grand Hotel

Limo

I'm sick of songs and I'm not joking.
Turn all singing into croaking!
Costumes tear and dancers stumble.
Make the audience groan and grumble.

To spoil each pop star's starry glee,
Take the fairy's objects three.
Hide them where they can't be found,
And silence every pretty sound!

The Sparkle
Sash

Contents

Christmas Angels

"I can't believe that we're really going to meet Serena, Emilia and Lexy!" Kirsty Tate said for the hundredth time that day.

"Neither can I!" smiled her best friend Rachel Walker.

Kirsty squeezed Rachel's hand as they stood in the entrance to their hotel suite with their parents. The girls had won a competition to meet their favourite girl band, The Angels. They were staying

11

overnight in The Grand Hotel and they were going to get a makeover from the band's stylists, help the band to turn on the city's Christmas lights and go to The Angels' Christmas charity concert the following evening!

"This is almost as exciting as one of our fairy adventures!"

Kirsty whispered to her best friend. No one else knew that they had a special friendship with the king and queen of Fairyland. Kirsty and Rachel had had many adventures with the fairies as they tried to stop mean Jack Frost and his naughty goblin servants from making mischief.

"This reminds me of the palace in Fairyland!" said Rachel, looking around with wide eyes. "It's so beautiful!"

"Oh, Rachel, look!" cried Kirsty. On a table in a corner of their room was the largest bunch of flowers the girls had ever seen, with a handwritten card on top.

Dear Kirsty and Rachel,
We hope you have a fun stay! We are really looking forward to meeting you later today. Serena, Emilia & Lexy
— The Angels xxx

While their parents unpacked, Kirsty and Rachel explored the enormous hotel suite. Their favourite room was the lounge. It was covered in red and gold Christmas decorations, and in the middle was a huge Christmas tree that filled the room with the scent of pine.

"Oh, Kirsty, look at the tiny bells hanging from the branches!" cried Rachel.

As she spoke, the tree seemed to shiver
and the little bells tinkled. Then a
burst of gold glitter cascaded
down from the angel on
top like a sparkling
waterfall. When
the whirl of
glitter stopped,
the girls saw a
beautiful fairy
sitting on a
piece of red
tinsel, waving
at them.

"Hello," she
said in a tinkling,
melodious voice.
"I'm Destiny the Pop
Star Fairy."

"It's wonderful to meet you!" exclaimed Kirsty.

"Thank you!" said Destiny with a dazzling smile. "It's lovely to meet you both too. I've heard so much about you from King Oberon and Queen Titania!"

"What are you doing in the city?" Rachel asked. "We're here because we won a competition."

"I know all about the competition," Destiny said. "That's why I'm here, too!"

"What do you mean?" asked Rachel.

"I need your help," Destiny said, her smile fading. "I look after the pop stars in the human world, and I am a pop singer in Fairyland too. Every year, there is a big Christmas concert in Fairyland. There is music and dancing, and spectacular

performances from some of the fairies. At the end, I always do a pop show. But now the whole concert may have to be cancelled."

"Oh no!" cried the girls. "Why?"

"Jack Frost decided that he wanted to perform the end-of-show number with his group," Destiny explained.

"Frosty and his Gobolicious Band?" cried Rachel. "But they're terrible!"

Rachel remembered how Jack Frost and his band had once tried to win the National Talent Competition. He had stolen the Music Fairies' Magical Musical Instruments, so that nobody could play music properly and his band would sound best. The girls and the Music Fairies had only just managed to stop him in time.

"Jack still thinks that he is the best singer in the whole of Fairyland," Destiny said. "He demanded top billing in the show."

"What did you do?" asked Kirsty.

"We let him audition," said Destiny,
"but his singing – and the band's playing
– was so awful that we couldn't say yes.
I told him to practise and audition
again next year, but he lost his temper
completely. He said that if he couldn't
be the star of the show, he would rid the
world of pop music completely!"

Jack Frost's Revenge

Rachel and Kirsty could hardly believe their ears.

"But how could Jack Frost get rid of all music?" Kirsty asked.

Destiny's shoulders sagged.

"I have three magical objects that are very important to Fairyland and to the human world," she said. "The Sparkle Sash protects pop stars' outfits and costumes. The Keepsake Key protects their songs and music, and the Magical Microphone ensures that the sound and lighting systems work smoothly. But Jack Frost has stolen all three magical objects. He's ordered his goblins to hide them here in the city, and to spoil The Angels' Christmas charity concert at the same time, just because they are the most successful pop group in the country!"

"So while the magical objects are missing, things will go wrong for pop groups in the human world?" Rachel asked.

Destiny nodded sadly.

"We can't let the charity concert be ruined," said Kirsty in a determined voice. "We just have to get those magical objects back before tomorrow night!"

"So you'll help me?" asked Destiny hopefully.

"Of course!" said Rachel and Kirsty together.

"I hoped you would say that!" said Destiny.

"When I heard that you had won the competition, I realised that you would be in exactly the right place to help."

"What do you want us to do?" asked Rachel eagerly.

"For the time being, just stay alert," said Destiny. "The goblins are somewhere in the city and they're bound to cause trouble sooner or later."

"We won't let those naughty goblins succeed," Rachel declared.

"Remember, keep a close eye on The Angels," Destiny added. "Jack Frost definitely wants to spoil things for them."

The girls nodded and Destiny disappeared with another explosion of gold glitter. Before the girls could speak, Mrs Tate came in to say that it was time to go to the stadium.

For the moment, all other thoughts flew out of Rachel's and Kirsty's minds. They were about to meet The Angels!

Mrs Walker and Mrs Tate rode in the limousine with Rachel and Kirsty, while their dads stayed behind at the hotel. When they reached the stadium they went to the backstage door, where a man with a clipboard and a headset was smiling and waving.

"Welcome to the Supersonic Stadium!" he said. "I'm here to take you to meet The Angels!"

He led the girls and their mums though the backstage door and down a long corridor lined with dressing rooms.

The last door had a
gold star with two
names printed inside it:

RACHEL WALKER
&
KIRSTY TATE

When the girls pushed
open the door, there
was a trio of excited squeals and then all
three of The Angels rushed over to hug
them. They were even prettier in real life
than they looked on the TV!

Emilia was tall and willowy, with big
green eyes and straight blonde hair that
swished around her oval face. She was
wearing a pair of blue skinny jeans and a
dark-red shrug over a sparkling camisole.

Serena had silky black hair and beautiful
brown eyes. She was wearing teal leggings
and a fitted tunic in swirling blues and
browns, with a wide brown belt sitting
loosely on her hips.

Lexy's sparkling blue eyes were full of fun. She had curling red-gold hair that flowed down her back, and she was wearing a simple green dress with knee-high tan boots.

"Welcome!" cried Emilia.

"Congratulations on winning the competition," said Serena with a smile.

"It's great to meet you!" Lexy added, her copper-coloured ringlets bouncing.

Mrs Tate and Mrs Walker went off to get a cup of tea, and The Angels told Rachel and Kirsty their plan for the day.

"You're going to get star treatment from our own stylists," Emilia began.

"And we'll give you a tour around the stadium," Serena put in.

"But *first* we are going to teach you the dance routine for our brand-new song!" Lexy finished eagerly.

The Glitter Trail

Half an hour later, Rachel and Kirsty were giggling with The Angels like old friends as they learned the dance steps.

"We did it!" Rachel cheered at last. "All the way through with no mistakes!"

They all hugged as the door opened and a man and a woman walked in.

"Girls, these are Rich and Charlotte, our stylist and make-up artist," said Emilia. "Rich can tell you what colours and styles suit you and Charlotte will give you a makeover!"

"Make-up should be subtle and simple," Charlotte said, pulling out a tube of sparkling lip gloss and a pot of silvery glitter.

The girls sat down in front of a mirror. As Charlotte dabbed glitter on to their

cheeks and eyelids, Rich talked about the colours that would suit them, and The Angels watched and chatted happily.

When Charlotte had finished, the girls went over to look at themselves in the full-length mirror on the back of the dressing-room door. Suddenly, Emilia's mobile phone started to ring.

As soon as she answered it, her face fell.

"But this could ruin the whole show!" she cried.

Rachel and Kirsty exchanged worried looks.

"That doesn't sound good," Kirsty said to Rachel.

"I wonder if Jack Frost has anything to do with it," Rachel murmured.

"That was our agent, Rowena," Emilia said as she hung up. "The lorry carrying our costumes has gone missing! Rowena can't reach the driver on his mobile and she has no idea where he is."

34

"But without the costumes, the show
will be really dull!" Lexy cried.

Rachel and Kirsty
were still standing
beside the door,
and suddenly
they heard the
pitter-patter
of running
footsteps in
the corridor
and a familiar,
squawking giggle.

"That sounded like goblins!" Kirsty
whispered urgently to Rachel. "They must
have the Sparkle Sash!"

Rich, Charlotte and The Angels were all
talking at once, and they weren't looking
at the girls.

"Let's go and see if we can find the goblins while they're talking," Rachel whispered.

The girls slipped out of the dressing room. Just down the corridor, a door was wide open.

"It's a storage room," said Kirsty, stepping inside. "Oh no!"

The room was a complete mess. Pots of face powder had been tipped out, dusting everything in a fine layer of pinks and bronzes.

HAIR ACCESSORIES

SPARE SHOES

36

The girls stared around in horror. Empty tubes of cream eye-shadow littered the floor, and the shimmering costumes on the clothes rail were smeared with purples, blues and golds. Face glitter was daubed on the walls and had been trodden into the carpet. "Look at this!" said Rachel in a grim tone. Someone had used red lipstick to draw a picture of Jack Frost on the wall with his tongue sticking out! "This is definitely the work of goblins!"

37

said Kirsty crossly.

Suddenly, Rachel grabbed Kirsty's arm.

"I think something is still in here!" she hissed, pointing into the far corner.

A long, silver boot was lying on the floor and shaking. It was much too small for a goblin, but *something* was definitely inside it!

"What is it?" cried Kirsty, stepping backwards.

The boot shook again, and then a jet of gold glitter shot out of the top, and Destiny appeared in front of the girls!

"Hi girls!" said the little fairy, looking in dismay at the mess in the room. "What's happened here?"

"It's the goblins," said Kirsty. "They're here! And the lorry full of The Angels' costumes has gone missing."

"Then we need to find the goblins quickly," said Destiny with a frown.

She waved her wand and there was a flurry of magical sparkles. When they cleared, the room was clean and tidy.

"Let's go and find the Sparkle Sash before the goblins cause any more trouble!" Destiny said.

She tucked herself into Kirsty's pocket and the girls hurried out into the corridor.

"Look!" cried Rachel, pointing at a trail of messy footprints on the floor. "These should lead us straight to the goblins!"

They followed the footprints along the corridor and through three sets of double doors, until at last they arrived at the back of the main stage.

Wires and leads were trailing across the floor and banks of switches stood all around them. Temporary steps led up to an archway, which was the entrance to the stage.

"Listen!" said Rachel softly.

There were horrible screeching sounds coming from the stage. Tiptoeing, Kirsty made her way up the steps, beckoning Rachel to follow her. Slowly they crept up and peered over the top.

Transparent steps led down to the main stage area, which was crowded with large floodlights, tall microphone stands...and five goblins prancing around the stage!

Showtime!

Kirsty and Rachel had to clamp their
hands over their mouths to stop themselves
laughing out loud. The goblins had raided
the storage cupboard and tried to dress
themselves as pop stars!

43

One goblin had a lime-green feather boa wound around his body. Another was wearing a thick layer of pink face powder and red blusher, with scarlet lipstick smeared all around his mouth. The other goblins were wearing silky shirts and sparkling hot pants, and one of them was swishing a long, clip-on hair extension that he had attached to his bony head.

They were singing into microphones…or rather, *trying* to sing.

"That's the worst noise I've ever heard!" cried Destiny, clapping her hands over her ears. "Thank goodness the microphones aren't switched on!"

"Look!" Kirsty exclaimed.

The smallest goblin had something wrapped around his waist – something long and gold that shimmered and glimmered in the stage lights.

"It's the Sparkle Sash!" Destiny exclaimed.

45

"But how can we get it away from the goblin?" Rachel asked.

Suddenly Kirsty smiled.

"I've got an idea!"

she said.
"Rachel,
can you
remember
the dance
routine that
The Angels
taught us?"

"I think
so," Rachel
said, nodding.

"Let's go and teach it to the goblins," Kirsty suggested, her eyes shining. "While they are concentrating on the steps, Destiny can take the sash!"

"It could work!" Rachel declared. "They'll all have to face in one direction and stay in one place. Destiny can fly up behind them without being seen!"

Rachel and Kirsty climbed up the steps and stood under the archway.

"Hi!" called Kirsty. "You must be the backing dancers. We're going to show you the new routine!"

One of the goblins giggled and nudged the others.

"They think we're humans!" he hissed loudly. "Our brilliant disguises have fooled them!"

47

The girls began to walk the goblins through the routine. They were *very* clumsy. *Crash!* They turned the wrong way and bashed into each other. *Bump!* They trod on each other's toes and hopped around, squealing. *Clatter!* They tripped over wires and knocked over all the microphone stands.

Amid the chaos, Destiny fluttered up behind the smallest goblin. As he pranced to the left and then to the right, the fairy flew closer and closer. Rachel and Kirsty held their breath. Could Destiny get the sash back before she was spotted?

Seizing the Sash

"And side-together-side, and reach for the stars!" Kirsty chanted.

The goblin wearing the Sparkle Sash was concentrating hard, with his tongue sticking out. He kept shaking his hips from side to side, and Destiny could not untie the sash.

"Keep your hips nice and still!" called Rachel.

Destiny gave Rachel a grateful wink and began to untie the Sparkle Sash with her delicate fingers. Slowly and gently, the little fairy slipped the sash away from the goblin's waist. At last it fell into her hands and she returned it to fairy size as she flitted away!

"Thank you!" Kirsty called out to the goblins, edging towards the staircase. "You have done very well. Carry on practising."

As they ran up the steps, the smallest goblin gave a yell of fury.

"My sash!" he shrieked, pointing a bony finger at the girls. "Thieves! They've stolen my sash!"

The girls froze on the staircase and Destiny flew over to join them, carrying the precious sash.

"*You* are the thieves!" she told the goblins indignantly. "I am going to return the Sparkle Sash to Fairyland, where it belongs!"

"We won't let you spoil The Angels' Christmas concert!" Rachel added bravely.

"Catch them!" squawked the plumpest goblin.

The goblins rushed towards the girls.

"Oh no you don't!" Destiny declared.

She waved her wand and a cloud of fairy dust surrounded the girls. As they blinked, they felt themselves becoming as small and delicate as Destiny, and fine, gossamer wings appeared on their backs. Fluttering their wings in delight, the girls rose into the air as the goblins charged towards them from all directions.

THUMP! The goblins bumped into each other and fell to the ground, screeching with rage. They immediately leapt up and sprang into the air, trying to reach the girls who were hovering just out

of reach. But because their eyes were on
the girls, they were not looking where
they were going. They ran blindly into
each other, squawking and yelling as they
knocked each other down and stumbled
over the lights and equipment on stage.

Destiny clapped her hands to get the
goblins' attention.

"You'd better go
and tell Jack Frost
that you've no
longer got
the sash,"
she said. "I
wouldn't like
to be in your
shoes when
he hears
the news!"

The goblins looked dejectedly at each other, and shuffled off towards the exit.

"Now I must clear up this mess," Destiny said, and, with a wave of her wand, the stage was back to normal.

Rachel, Kirsty and Destiny flew back to the corridor and into the storage room. Destiny was still holding the precious Sparkle Sash.

"Thank you so much for your help, girls," Destiny said, happily

pressing the sash to her heart. "I could never have got this back without you."

They all hugged, and then Destiny waved her wand again and returned Rachel and Kirsty to their human size.

"Are you going to take the sash back to Fairyland now?" asked Kirsty.

Destiny nodded.

"The sooner it's back in its rightful place, the better!" she declared. "Goodbye, girls. I'll see you again soon!"

Rachel and Kirsty waved as Destiny disappeared in a whirl of sparkles. Then Rachel squeezed Kirsty's hand.

"Come on!" she said. "Let's go back to The Angels!"

In the dressing room, Rachel and Kirsty found The Angels hugging and jumping around in excitement. Lexy saw the girls and rushed over to embrace them.

"The lorry has been found!" she squealed happily, dancing around the room with them. "The driver's satnav sent him to a duck farm in the middle of the countryside! Then his lorry broke down and he couldn't ring us because his mobile battery was

flat. But at the last minute a breakdown truck drove past and rescued him, and then his satnav started working again. Can you believe it?"

"The costumes are all safe," said Emilia. "So now we can relax and give you that tour of the stadium we promised you. Come on, girls!"

As they set off, Rachel and Kirsty shared a secret smile. Now there were only two magical objects left to find.

"Isn't it amazing that the truck was found so quickly?" said Serena, linking arms with the girls as they walked off.

Kirsty and Rachel looked at each other and giggled.

"It's just like magic!" said Kirsty.

The Keepsake Key

Contents

Shopping Like Stars

Over breakfast the next morning,
Mr Tate had a surprise for the girls.

"We thought you would like some
new outfits to wear to the concert, so
we're taking you shopping at Harwoods,"
he said.

"That's the most famous department
store in the whole city!" gasped Rachel,
her eyes sparkling. "How exciting!"

But when the adults started talking about how to get to Harwoods, Kirsty whispered in Rachel's ear.

"What about the Keepsake Key?" she said. "I really want to visit Harwoods, but we must help Destiny get her other two magical objects back before Jack Frost and his goblins ruin pop music forever!"

"Queen Titania always says that we should let the magic come to us," Rachel said thoughtfully. "I think we should go to Harwoods, but look out for anything that might lead us to the goblins and the Keepsake Key."

"You're right," Kirsty said. "Oh Rachel, I can't wait to see what Harwoods is really like!"

The Harwoods building was magnificent. It was made of gleaming white marble and was surrounded by tall pillars. Flags bearing the Harwoods logo fluttered above every entrance, and tall doormen in blue uniforms held the heavy glass doors open for the girls and their families.

Rachel and Kirsty felt very excited as they travelled up the long escalators to the third floor. The women and girls' fashion department was huge. As their parents headed off in one direction, Rachel and Kirsty hurried eagerly towards a rack that was full of clothes in all the colours of the rainbow. Kirsty pulled out a pretty red skirt and a fitted white top with a sparkly red star on the front.

"This would look great with some glittery ballet pumps!" she said.

Suddenly, a small child ran past them and nearly pushed Rachel over into the clothes rail. "Hey!' cried Kirsty. "You should be more careful!"

But the child took no notice. He or she was wearing a hooded top, and ran over to join two other hooded children. They began pushing each other and yelling.

"I'm OK," said Rachel, turning back to look at the clothes again. "That skirt is just right, Kirsty. It's red – the colour that Rich and Charlotte said suits you best. You should try it on!"

"First we have to find something for

you!" said Kirsty with a smile. "Rich said that blue would be your best colour."

They looked through the racks, pulling out clothes and holding them up against each other. Suddenly Kirsty gave a cry of excitement.

"Perfect!" she said triumphantly.

She had found a pair of dark blue jeans with a sequin trim on the back pockets and the waistline, and a bright blue wrapover top covered in tiny sequins and sparkles. Rachel clapped her hands together.

"Amazing!" she declared. "Kirsty, I think you're as good a stylist as Rich!"

Just then there was a loud, squawking
shout from the dresses section. The
naughty children were now parading
around the shop in expensive evening
dresses. Their heads were swathed in silky
scarves, and one of them had just trodden
on another's trailing gown.

"What noisy children!"
said Mr Tate, walking
up behind the girls.
"I wonder
where their
parents are."

"I haven't
seen any
grown-ups
with them,"
commented
Rachel.

"Hmm, it's odd to see children running around on their own like that," said Kirsty thoughtfully.

"Ah, I see you've found some outfits," said Mrs Walker.

"You'd better try them on," said Mrs Tate.

The best friends walked into the changing room and chose a cubicle. As they tried on their new outfits, Kirsty leaned closer to Rachel.

"I think those naughty children might actually be goblins!" she said in a whisper. "They keep hiding their faces, they're the right size, and there are no adults with them."

Rachel nodded in agreement.

"We need to find out what they're up to," she said. "But we can't follow them – our parents are right outside!"

They stood side by side and looked into the large mirror. The outfits looked great, but now they had more important things to think about!

"Let's tell our parents that we've chosen these outfits and then we'll try to get closer to the goblins," said Kirsty.

Rachel nodded and they changed into their own clothes again. Kirsty bent down to tie up her shoelace...and then froze.

Very slowly she looked up at Rachel and beckoned. As Rachel bent down, Kirsty pointed.

Poking out from the bottom of the next-door cubicle was a pair of large, green feet!

Goblin Fashion

"Now that is definitely a goblin!" Rachel hissed.

"Right," said Kirsty in a firm voice. "Come on!"

The girls stepped out of the cubicle and Kirsty pulled open the curtain of the one next to them.

The goblin inside didn't notice them at first. He was too busy preening himself in the full-length mirror. He was wearing a purple velvet suit and a rainbow-striped waistcoat. As they watched, he raised a trilby hat to his head and put it on at a jaunty angle.

Kirsty and Rachel burst out laughing at the sight of the vain little goblin! He whirled around and gave an embarrassed yelp of surprise. His green cheeks went red.

"You horrible girls!" he stammered.
"How dare you
laugh at me!
I'm the most
fashionable
goblin that
ever was!"

He stuck out
his tongue and
darted past them
in a rage.

"Quickly," said Kirsty, trying to stop
giggling, "we have to follow him!"

The girls dashed after the goblin, but
they ran straight into their parents, who
had been waiting outside the changing
rooms on luxurious sofas.

"So, did you like the outfits?" asked Mrs
Walker.

"We loved them," said Rachel.

"Wonderful!" said Mrs Tate. "Let's pay for them, and then we can look for shoes."

Kirsty and Rachel exchanged desperate glances as the goblin disappeared behind a clothing display. They would have to give up the chase…for now.

The shoe department was up on the next floor. As the girls and their parents rode up the escalator, Rachel and Kirsty spotted three small figures dressed in bright clothes and wearing long wigs.

One had bouncing black ringlets, another had sleek blonde locks, and the third was now a fiery redhead. They were running up the down escalator, losing their balance and shrieking with laughter. Shoppers were leaping out of their way and pressing themselves against the side of the escalator.

Suddenly, the black-haired goblin fell
over the side of the escalator onto the one
going the other way. He began wailing
as he rode up the escalator away from his
friends.

"Jump off!" shouted the blonde goblin,
riding down to the bottom and staring
upwards.

"No, stay on and then come down
the other way!" shouted the redhead,
joining him.

The black-haired goblin began to
run down the up escalator, puffing and
panting, while the other two shouted
words of encouragement.

"You can do it!"

"Faster!"

He put on an extra burst of speed, lost his balance and tumbled head over heels to the bottom of the escalator. He landed at the feet of a cross-looking security guard in a blue-and-silver uniform.

"What's going on here, then?" the security guard demanded.

"*Run away!*" shrieked the blonde goblin.

The goblins scattered as the security guard began to chase them. They dashed into the music department.

"We must follow them!" whispered
Kirsty to Rachel. The girls chose their
new shoes very
quickly, and
a few minutes
later they
were queuing
up to pay.

"After
all that
shopping,
I could do with a cup of tea," said Mr
Tate. "Shall we go to the café on the top
floor?"

"Good idea!" said the other adults.

"I'm not thirsty," Rachel said. "Are
you, Kirsty? If not, perhaps we could go
and look around the music department
instead?"

"Yes, all right," said Mrs Walker. "We'll meet you in the café when you've finished looking around."

"Come on," said Kirsty in a low voice, as she and Rachel headed away from the adults. "We have to stop those goblins causing any more mischief – and find out if they have the Keepsake Key!"

"Look at that mirror!" said Rachel suddenly.

She pointed at a mirror by their feet.

They had been using it to see the shoes they were trying on. But now it wasn't reflecting the girls' feet; it was shimmering and sparkling with gold and red light.

"Oh Rachel," whispered Kirsty. "It's fairy magic!"

The Missing Music

The girls dropped on their knees beside the mirror. It began to ripple, like water after a pebble has been thrown into it. Rachel and Kirsty caught a glimpse of pink turrets and blue sky – and then a small figure filled the mirror and burst through in a flurry of golden sparkles and musical notes. It was Destiny!

"Hello, girls!" she said. "Any sign of the Keepsake Key?"

"Destiny, it's wonderful to see you!" Rachel smiled.

"You're just in time," Kirsty added. "The goblins are here in Harwoods causing lots of trouble!"

"We were about to follow them to the music department," said Rachel. "But it's hard to keep them in sight."

"Well, let's see what we can do about that," said Destiny with a smile.

She waved her wand and in a flurry of fairy dust the girls had shrunk to fairy size, complete with glittering, gauzy wings.

"Thank you!" said
Rachel, fluttering
her delicate
wings and doing
a somersault in
the air. "They
won't spot us so
easily now!"

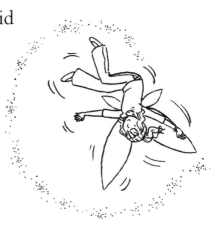

"This way!" said Destiny, pointing
towards the next department. "I have
something to show you, and the electrical
department is the perfect place to do it."

They fluttered towards the electrical
department, taking care to keep out of
sight of other shoppers. Destiny waved her
wand at a bank of flickering TV screens
in front of them. There was a golden
crackle on the screens, and an image
of The Angels appeared on every one.

They were in their dressing room, looking very upset.

"It's true," Emilia was saying. "Every single copy of the sheet music for *Key to My Heart* has disappeared!"

"But it's our new charity single," groaned Serena. "We've got to sing it at the concert tonight, or nobody will buy it and the charity won't get any money."

"Without the sheet music, none of the backing singers and musicians will be able to perform," said Lexy. "What are we going to do?"

The images faded, and Destiny looked sadly at Rachel and Kirsty.

"This isn't a coincidence," she said. "The Keepsake Key protects pop stars' songs and music. Without it, everything will go wrong for The Angels...and their favourite charity won't get a penny!"

"We're not going to let Jack Frost spoil everything," said Kirsty in a determined tone. "Come on, let's find those goblins and *make* them give back the Keepsake Key!"

Hide and Seek

When they reached the music
department, everything seemed calm
and quiet.

"Perhaps they've gone to another
department," Kirsty suggested.

"No – listen!" said Rachel.

The girls could hear a rhythmic squeaking sound in the distance. It grew louder and louder, until around the corner sped a unicycle with a squeaky wheel, ridden by a goblin wearing a long chiffon dress. Close behind him was another goblin on a pogo stick, wearing a pair of heart-patterned pyjamas and a curly blonde wig that bounced around his ears as he jumped. A third goblin was wobbling along on roller blades,

wearing a swimming costume and a
bobble hat.

"More goblins!" cried Kirsty.

"Look at what that goblin on the pogo
stick has on a chain around his neck,"
Destiny said, tingling with excitement.
"It's my Keepsake Key!"

The goblin with the key was looking
very bad-tempered. The girls and Destiny
fluttered closer to hear what he was
saying, carefully staying out of sight.

"Stop telling me what to do!"
he was whining to the other goblins.
"I'll hide the
key later –
right now I
want to play
on my pogo
stick!"

"But *where*
are we going
to hide it?"
demanded
another goblin.
"We've been all over the store
looking for the perfect hiding place, and
all we've found are those pesky human
girls!"

As the goblins argued, Rachel leaned
over to Kirsty and Destiny.

"I think I could unfasten the chain
from his neck and fly away with it," she
whispered.

"Oh, be careful!," said Destiny
anxiously.

Rachel flew up behind the goblin,
ducking down behind his shoulders so
that the other goblins didn't see her. She
reached up to unfasten the chain, but one
of her wings brushed against his green
skin.

"Something's
tickling my
neck!" he
exclaimed,
whirling around.
"Look! A fairy
is trying to steal
the key!"

He yanked the chain from around
his neck and tucked the key
inside his
pyjama pocket.

"Run away!"
bellowed the
goblin on roller
blades.

The three
goblins zoomed
into the next
department and
Destiny and the girls flitted after them,
but they stopped just inside the entrance.
The department was full of children...and
they were the same size as the goblins!

"It's the toy department!" Rachel
groaned. "How are we ever going to
find three little goblins in here?

"Let's fly close to the ceiling for a better view," suggested Destiny.

They fluttered up to the ceiling of the toy department. There were crowds of children gathered around the low tables piled high with toys. But there was no sign of the goblins.

"It's no use," sighed Destiny. "We'll never find them!"

Suddenly there was a familiar shriek from the other side of the room.

"That's a goblin!" Rachel exclaimed.

They flew towards the sound, being careful to stay out of sight, and saw the three goblins staring in fear at a guide dog. It was a gentle golden retriever and it wasn't paying any attention to the goblins, but their knobbly green knees were knocking together.

"Help!" squealed the goblin in the blonde wig. "It's huge!"

He leapt into the arms of the second goblin.

"I don't like hairy monsters either!" squeaked the second goblin, leaping into the arms of the third goblin, who shrieked and collapsed under the weight.

"Those silly goblins!" said Rachel as the dog and his owner walked away. "Guide dogs are the gentlest dogs in the world."

Destiny giggled, but Kirsty was looking thoughtful.

"If they're so scared of dogs, perhaps there's another way to get the Keepsake Key back," she said. "Did you see those battery-powered dogs?"

"Yes," said Rachel eagerly. "They're in a wooden pen in the middle of the department."

"Perhaps the goblins won't realise that they are just toys!" said Kirsty.

"And they might forget about the Keepsake Key if they are distracted by the dogs!" said Destiny, "Kirsty, that's a wonderful idea!"

Scaredy-Goblins!

"Let's go after one goblin each," said Rachel. "We can try to drive them towards the pen."

"But what about the children in the department?" Kirsty asked. "We can't let them see us."

"I can use my magic to distract them for a few minutes," Destiny said.

She waved her wand and a cloud of magical sparkles danced through the air, which turned into hundreds of coloured balloons. A sparkly banner appeared on the other side of the department.

FREE BALLOONS!

Shouts and whoops of delight went up from the children as they followed the beautiful

balloons. Within seconds, the area around the toy dog pen was completely deserted.

The plan worked perfectly. By flitting up and down the aisles of toys, the girls shepherded the goblins closer and closer to the wooden pen. At last they all charged forwards and the goblins collided with a tremendous CRASH! They tumbled head over heels – *straight into the wooden pen!*

The goblins sat up and shook their heads dizzily, surrounded by yapping, flipping toy dogs.

"EEEK!"
squealed the
blonde-wigged
goblin, trying
to clamber
on top of
the second
goblin.
"Lots
of hairy
monsters!"

"Help!" cried the third goblin,
"Save me!"

"Get off!" wailed the second goblin.

"Goblins!" said Destiny, fluttering
above the pen. "I want you to return the
Keepsake Key."

"No way!" squeaked the smallest
goblin.

At that moment one of the toy dogs yapped loudly and flipped over, landing on the lap of one of the goblins.

"I think I'm going to faint!" whimpered the goblin.

"If you give me the key, I'll make sure you're safe," said Destiny, folding her arms. "Well?"

"Just give her the key!" trembled the goblin. "I don't want to get eaten!"

111

The blonde-wigged goblin pulled the Keepsake Key out of his pocket and threw it to Destiny, who shrank it down to fairy-size and caught it neatly.

"Those 'monsters' are just toys!" she said, rising high into the air. "Now you must stop causing trouble and leave the store!"

"What?" roared the smallest goblin. "You tricksy fairies!"

"This is your fault!" shouted the third goblin to the one with the blonde wig. "You and that stupid pogo stick!"

He yanked the blonde wig off the other's head and jumped up and down on top of it.

"I'm going home!" he said grumpily.

He stomped out of the toy department, followed by the other goblins.

113

Destiny and the girls fluttered back into the electrical department beside the TV screens. They were so excited that they had outsmarted the goblins!

"I can't thank you enough," Destiny said as she hugged them both. "I have to take the key back to Fairyland so that The Angels find their music in time, but I'll come back as soon as I can. We have to find the Magical Microphone!"

"We'll be ready and waiting," Rachel promised.

Destiny smiled and waved her wand over the girls, returning them to human size. Then she disappeared in a shower of glitter and musical notes.

After a few seconds, there was a golden crackle and a picture of The Angels appeared on the television screens. They were laughing and hugging.

"Found in the nick of time!" Emilia declared, waving a sheaf of sheet music in the air.

The girls smiled happily at each other
as the picture faded. Then
Rachel glanced at
the clock on
the wall and
gasped.

"Kirsty,
there
are only
four more
hours until the
Christmas lights
are switched on!" she exclaimed.

"Followed by the charity concert!"
added Kirsty. "Oh Rachel, if we can't
find the Magical Microphone, Jack Frost
could still ruin the concert for everyone
by making the sound *and* lighting systems
go wrong."

"Don't worry, Kirsty, I'm sure we'll find the Magical Microphone in time," Rachel said. "After all, we've got Destiny to help us. If anyone can find it, we can!"

The Magical Microphone

Contents

The Return of Jack Frost

Rachel and Kirsty's thoughts whirled as they got changed, ready for the switching on of the Christmas lights and the charity concert. They felt excited and worried at the same time. Jack Frost had tried to spoil things by stealing Destiny the Pop Star Fairy's three magical objects, and although the girls had got back the Sparkle Sash and the Keepsake Key, the Magical Microphone was still missing!

"Look at the stars twinkling in the sky," said Kirsty, pressing her nose against the hotel-room window and gazing up. "It's a lovely evening."

"I'm glad," said Rachel, joining her at the window. "The switching on of the lights might be cancelled if it rained!"

"Hurry up, girls!" called Mrs Tate from outside their room. "The Angels will be here soon."

Kirsty looked at the clock on the wall. "Oh Rachel, it's nearly time," she said. "And there's still no sign of the Magical Microphone!"

"I know," said Rachel, looking solemn, "but I'm sure we'll find it. We mustn't let Jack Frost spoil things by making us worry. Just think, Kirsty, tonight we'll be helping The Angels to turn on the city's Christmas lights! Can you believe it?"

"No!" said Kirsty, grinning at her best friend. "I've seen it on TV so many times, it just doesn't seem real that we're going to be part of it!"

"Come on, girls!" called Mrs Tate again.

Rachel and Kirsty smiled at each other in excitement, then pulled on their coats and hurried out.

The Angels were waiting for the girls in the hotel lobby. They waved when they saw Rachel and Kirsty.

"Have a wonderful time, girls," said Mrs Walker, kissing them both. "We'll see you later, after the ceremony!"

Their parents left to make their own way to Main Street, and Rachel and Kirsty rushed over to The Angels.

"Girls, you look great!" said Serena, giving them each a hug. "Come on, our car's here!"

They led the girls out of the hotel. A long, pink Cadillac was waiting outside, with a smart chauffeur at the wheel.

Feeling like pop stars themselves, Rachel and Kirsty climbed in and snuggled into the soft, cream

seats. The Angels joined them, and then the Cadillac purred away.

"We're really excited about turning on the lights," Emilia told them. "It's such a special occasion."

"Lots of people wear fancy dress and there's a great party atmosphere," Lexy added eagerly. "It's a bit like a carnival!"

Serena laughed and pointed at a scooter
that was riding alongside them in the
traffic.

"See what we mean?" she giggled.

Kirsty and Rachel looked at the scooter,
and their mouths fell open in surprise. Six

goblins were standing
on the back in a
pyramid shape,
just like stunt
riders. They were
waving their
arms around
to try to
keep their
balance, and
looking very
unsteady and
nervous.

"Oh no!" groaned Kirsty in a low voice. "Rachel, look at the driver!"

Spikes of silvery blue icicles were poking out from underneath the driver's helmet. It was Jack Frost!

As Rachel clutched Kirsty's arm in alarm, Jack Frost turned and gave them

a horrible, mocking smile. Then he held up a glittering golden microphone.

"The Magical Microphone!" whispered Rachel in Kirsty's ear. "And there's no way we can get it!"

"If only Destiny were here," Kirsty groaned.

With a final flourish of the microphone and a cackling laugh, Jack Frost picked up speed and roared away. He wound in and out of the busy traffic, with the goblins clinging on for dear life.

Suddenly, the goblin at the top gave a massive wobble. He flapped his arms madly, looking as if he were trying to fly, but it was no use. As the girls watched in horror, he lost his balance, fell off the scooter and landed on the road – right in the middle of the traffic!

Destiny to the Rescue!

The goblin leapt to his feet as quick as a flash, but the scooter was already almost out of sight. Furiously, the goblin jumped up and down in the middle of the road and shook his fist after the disappearing pyramid of goblins.

"It's lucky that everyone wears fancy dress for the ceremony," said Kirsty in a low voice. "People will think he's in a costume."

Car horns hooted at the angry goblin, and he shook his fist at them too. Then he spotted a bus and jumped on board. The girls saw him settle moodily into a seat, folding his arms and looking very bad-tempered.

Luckily, The Angels hadn't noticed anything. They were practising their harmonies for the concert that evening, and the car was filled with their sweet, clear voices. Normally, Kirsty and Rachel would have been thrilled to hear this private performance, but now they just felt worried about the Magical Microphone.

"We have to tell Destiny that Jack Frost is here," Rachel whispered in Kirsty's ear.

"I know," said Kirsty. "But how? She can't appear to us here, because The Angels would see her."

Suddenly the soft purr of the Cadillac's engine was replaced by a banging, rattling sound. The car began to jerk and judder, and then it came to a stop in the middle of the road.

The Angels stopped singing and looked around in alarm.

"That doesn't sound good," said Lexy.

"We're going to be late for the ceremony!" Serena cried.

The chauffeur got out and opened the bonnet. A cloud of steam hissed out and he coughed and waved his hand to clear the air.

"Let's go and see if we can help," said Emilia. "Girls, you stay here. Hopefully this won't take long!"

The Angels got out of the car and joined the chauffeur as he peered at the engine. With the bonnet raised up, neither the Angels nor the chauffeur could see into the car, which was lucky, because...

"Oh Kirsty, look!" Rachel cried in excitement.

The gear stick was glowing and sparkling. Then, with a burst of miniature fireworks in the shape of musical notes, the top of it flipped open like a lid. A platform rose out of it with Destiny right in the middle!

"Destiny!" cried Rachel and Kirsty together.

"Hi girls!" said the fairy with a dazzling smile.

"Jack Frost is here in the human world!" Kirsty blurted out, her words tumbling over themselves.

"Oh no!" Destiny exclaimed. "Where is he now?"

The girls explained what they had seen.

"We have to follow him!" cried Destiny at once.

"Yes, but right now we're not going anywhere," said Rachel, waving her arm towards the open bonnet. "The car has broken down!"

"And The Angels are supposed to be turning on the Christmas lights very soon," Kirsty added urgently. "If they can't get there, the ceremony will be ruined!"

"This is all because the Magical Microphone is still missing," Destiny said with a frown. "You see, it keeps things working smoothly around pop stars, but in the wrong hands it could make all sorts of technical things go wrong. That could mean failing sound equipment, faulty lighting..."

"Or broken car engines?" Rachel finished.

"Exactly," Destiny said, nodding. "But I can fix that!"

She flitted over to land delicately on Rachel's shoulder. Then she waved her wand towards the front of the car, and a healthy, purring roar came from the engine.

"Hurray!" cried Rachel and Kirsty, clapping their hands together.

Destiny quickly hid inside Rachel's bag.

Looking very relieved,

The Angels and the chauffeur jumped
back into the car, and they set off again.
Rachel and Kirsty watched the clock
anxiously. Could they reach Main Street
in time for the ceremony?

City of Surprises

The car arrived at Main Street with only a minute to spare, and The Angels and Rachel and Kirsty jumped out and hurried up the steps to the podium. The waiting crowds cheered and the Mayor smiled in relief.

"Keep a look out for Jack Frost!" said Destiny, peeping out of the top of Rachel's bag.

Rachel and Kirsty didn't need to be told to do that! Their eyes scanned the packed crowd, searching for any sign of Jack Frost's spiky head.

The Angels stood in front of the microphone and waved at their fans. Beside the microphone was the big red button that would turn on the Christmas lights.

"We are thrilled to have been asked to turn on the city's Christmas lights this year," Serena began. "It's such an honour to..."

As she continued her speech, Kirsty gripped Rachel's hand in excitement.

"I see him!" she exclaimed.

Jack Frost was standing at the edge of the crowd. Before the girls could think what to do, he stuck out his tongue and then tapped his wand against the Magical Microphone.

Immediately, all the streetlights and all the lights in the shops went out. Main Street was plunged into darkness! Gasps and cries went up from the crowd, and the girls heard the Mayor stumbling towards the microphone. He tapped it, but it wasn't working.

"Don't panic!" he shouted as loudly as he could. "Everyone keep still! Just a technical hitch, that's all!" He turned to his assistant and added in a low voice, "Find out what's wrong and fix it – quickly!"

Destiny quickly flew out of Rachel's bag.

"Keep still," she said. "I'm going to turn you into fairies!"

The girls didn't see her wand move, but they felt themselves shrinking to fairy-size and filmy wings growing on their backs.

"Take my hands," Destiny whispered.

Rachel and Kirsty stretched out their hands in the darkness, and felt Destiny's fingers intertwine with theirs. Then they fluttered their wings, rose into the air and flew to where Jack Frost had been standing.

When they left Main Street, they found
that the lights were still on in the side
streets. Almost at once, Rachel's bright
eyes spotted a skinny
green leg
disappearing
into the stage
door of
a theatre.

"In there!"
she cried.

The girls
zoomed towards the door and zipped into
the theatre.

Inside, the lights were down and a
musical was in full swing. The girls
paused in dismay – the loud singing was
drowning out any sound of giggling
goblins that they might have followed.

They even had to shout to hear each other.

"Let's fly over the rows one by one and search," Kirsty yelled.

They split up and began a methodical search of the theatre, from the front to the back. No one saw them because it was so  dark, and all eyes were on the stage. Just as the song finished, Kirsty grabbed the others' hands and pointed. Jack Frost was sitting in the very back row with five goblins!

They all had large bags of sweets open on their laps and their feet were resting on the backs of the seats in front. They were making so much noise that they were disturbing everyone around them. The goblins were noisily unwrapping sweets and making sucking, squelching sounds as they shoved the sweets into their mouths. Jack Frost was heckling the actors by shouting "Boo!" and

"Rubbish!" as he helped himself to the goblins' sweets. The goblins hadn't quite grasped the idea of heckling. One just kept yelling "Rhubarb!" Another was shouting, "Heckle! Heckle!", and the remaining three were bawling, "It's behind you!" at the actors on the stage. "Those naughty goblins!" cried Destiny in distress. "They're spoiling the show for everyone!"

Musical Mayhem

"They haven't seen us," said Kirsty. "Let's creep up and try to find the Magical Microphone without them noticing."

"Good idea," said Rachel. "They must think they've given us the slip."

They flitted carefully towards the back row. Closer...closer...until at last they were right behind Jack Frost's seat.

"Look!" whispered Destiny.

Underneath his seat, lit up by the pale aisle lights, was the shining Magical Microphone!

"All we have to do is reach out and take it," said Rachel breathlessly.

Ever so slowly and quietly, the three friends stretched their hands towards the microphone...and then they heard a nasty

chuckle above them. Jack Frost was peering over the back of his seat, and pointing his wand at them!

"Oh, I don't think so, little fairies!" he said gloatingly. "You'll never get the better of me!"

Kirsty opened her mouth to respond, but she never got the chance. The doors of the theatre crashed open and revealed a wet, muddy green figure wearing a crash helmet.

"YOU LEFT ME BEHIND!" he bellowed.

It was the goblin who had fallen off the scooter! He was covered in mud, dripping with water and boiling with rage as he pointed a bony finger at the other goblins.

"I've been thrown off a bus because I didn't have a ticket," he screeched. "I've been pushed into muddy puddles, squashed by late-night shoppers and nearly trampled by a police horse, and it's *all your fault!*"

He flung himself at the other goblins and the back row suddenly became a seething mass of green arms and legs. Squeals and yells filled the air.

Jack Frost hadn't taken his eyes off the
girls. He wasn't going to let them take
the Magical Microphone while his back
was turned! But because his attention was
on Rachel, Kirsty and Destiny, he didn't
see the angry faces of the people in the
row in front, turning around to glare at
him. He didn't see them rising out of their
seats and calling the stewards over, and
he didn't see the stewards arriving and
reaching out to grab the goblins and their
master!

"Hey!" yelled
Jack Frost as a
steward took
hold of him,
pinning his
arms to his
sides.

"Lemme go!"
wailed the muddy,
screeching goblin
as another
steward seized
him by the
shoulders.

The goblins
and their
master writhed
and yelled, but
the stewards held
them firmly.

"I don't care how much effort you've
put into these silly costumes," hissed
the chief steward furiously. "We're not
putting up with this noise a moment
longer. We're removing you from the
theatre!"

Jack Frost turned towards the girls, who had ducked out of sight. He struggled to get his wand arm free so that he could cast an icy spell, but the steward was bigger than him. Three stewards marched out of the theatre with an angry, kicking goblin under each arm, led by the chief steward holding Jack Frost in a grip of iron.

"You'll regret this!" Jack Frost bellowed.

His wails faded away as he and the goblins were thrown out of the building, and the girls stared at each other in shocked delight. Jack Frost was gone, but the Magical Microphone was *still under the seat!*

Destiny waved her wand and a rush of glittering fairy dust returned the Magical Microphone to her hands and to its Fairyland size.

"Hurry!" said Kirsty, rising into the air. "Let's get back to Main Street as fast as we can. We have to save the ceremony!"

The Christmas Concert

A minute later, Rachel and Kirsty landed back on the podium in Main Street, next to The Angels. The technicians were still trying to fix the lights, and the crowd was starting to grumble.

Destiny flung her arms around the girls.

"I can never thank you enough for helping me!" she said, her voice bubbling with happiness. "Everything will be all right for The Angels and the charity concert now. I must hurry back to Fairyland to return the Magical Microphone – and get ready for my own concert!"

And with a sprinkle of fairy dust, Destiny returned the girls to their normal size.

"I'll see you again soon!" Destiny whispered in their ears.

"Goodbye!" they whispered back.

Then she was gone, and seconds later, all the lights came back on. The crowd cheered and laughed, as Rachel and Kirsty blinked and looked around.

"A bit of drama adds to the fun!" joked Emilia, stepping up to the microphone to speak. "Ladies and gentlemen, girls and boys, all we really want to say is..."

Serena, Lexy, Rachel and Kirsty joined her in front of the microphone and put their hands over the big red button.

"Merry Christmas, everyone!" they shouted together.

They all pressed the button, and the Christmas lights burst into life, illuminating Main Street and filling every corner with colour and light. As the crowd cheered, The Angels were whisked away to get ready for their concert. The girls' parents were waiting beside the limousine that would take them all to the Supersonic Stadium.

When they arrived at the stadium, the audience was buzzing with feverish anticipation. Kirsty and Rachel felt their hearts thumping with excitement as they took their seats in the VIP area and waited for the performance to begin.

It was a spectacular concert. The audience was dancing in the aisles after the first song, and when The Angels sang their biggest hit, the cheers and screams were so loud that the girls could hardly hear the song! But the real highlight of the show was their new charity release, *Key to My Heart* .

At the end of the concert, Rachel and Kirsty went backstage to say goodbye to The Angels and thank them for a wonderful couple of days.

After they had hugged Emilia, Lexy and Serena, they and their parents stepped into the waiting limousine for the last time.

The girls couldn't get the catchy new song out of their heads, and they sang it all the way back to the hotel.

"You're always there to hold my hand,
You stand by me, you understand.
When I'm with you I feel so glad,
The truest friend I ever had.
I know we two will never part,
And that's the real key to my heart!"

"Oh, I'm so sleepy!" said Rachel with a big yawn as they changed into their pyjamas in the hotel room.

"Me too," said Kirsty, throwing back the covers to climb into bed. "Oh, Rachel – look!"

On her pillow was a lovely silver hand mirror.

"I've got one too!" cried Rachel.

The girls picked up the mirrors and turned them over. On the back of each one was a delicate inscription that said, 'With love and thanks, Destiny xx'. They turned them over again, and then gasped with delight. When they looked into the glass, they could see Destiny waving at them, with King Oberon and Queen Titania behind her.

"Thank you, Rachel and Kirsty!"

Destiny said. "The concert was a wonderful success and it's all thanks to you!"

"We're so glad!" Rachel whispered. "Goodnight, everyone! We hope to see you again soon!"

The girls snuggled down into their beds and smiled sleepily at each other.

"We've had lots of exciting, magical adventures," murmured Kirsty. "But you know what, Rachel? I think that this has definitely been the most star-studded one yet!"

The Ocean Fairies

Now it's time for Kirsty and Rachel to
help The Ocean Fairies! The first fairy
they meet is

Ally the Dolphin Fairy

Off to Fairyland

Kirsty Tate and Rachel Walker stepped off the bus and blinked in the sunshine. The two girls were staying with Kirsty's gran in Leamouth for the spring holiday and today they'd come to Lea-on-Sea, a small seaside resort along the coast. "I've got some shopping to do, so I'll meet you back here at midday," Kirsty's gran said, getting off the bus. "Have fun!"

"We will," Kirsty assured her. "See you later, Gran." Then she turned to Rachel. "Come on, let's go down to the beach!"

It took the girls just moments to walk down the sandy steps to the curving bay, which was packed with families enjoying the sun. The sky was a clear, fresh blue, and a breeze ruffled the tops of the waves. Lots of children were paddling in the sea, while shrieking seagulls soared above them, their strong white wings stretched wide.

"It's lovely," Rachel said, slipping off her shoes and wiggling her bare toes in the warm sand. She pointed to the far edge of the bay. "Let's go over there, shall we? It's a bit less crowded."

The girls made their way across the beach, zigzagging between deck chairs, wind-breaks and sandcastles. Then Kirsty stopped walking suddenly and bent down. "Hey, look at this shell," she said, picking it up to show Rachel. "It's really sparkly..."

Win Rainbow Magic goodies!

There are seven stars in
Destiny the Pop Star Fairy and every one has
a secret letter in it. Find all seven letters and rearrange
them to make a special Fairyland word, then send it to
us. Each month we will put the entries into a draw and
select one winner to receive a Rainbow Magic Sparkly
T-shirt and Goody Bag!

Send your entry on a postcard to Rainbow Magic
Destiny Competition, Orchard Books, 338 Euston
Road, London NW1 3BH. Australian readers should
write to Hachette Children's Books, Level 17/207 Kent
Street, Sydney, NSW 2000.

New Zealand readers should write to Rainbow
Magic Competition, 4 Whetu Place, Mairangi Bay,
Auckland, NZ. Don't forget to include your name
and address. Only one entry per child.
Final draw: 29th October 2010.

Good luck!

Meet the
Ocean Fairies
in April 2010

Ally the Dolphin Fairy
978-1-40830-815-8

Amelie the Seal Fairy
978-1-40830-816-5

Pia the Penguin Fairy
978-1-40830-817-2

Tess the Sea Turtle Fairy
978-1-40830-818-9

Stephanie the Starfish Fairy
978-1-40830-819-6

Whitney the Whale Fairy
978-1-40830-820-2

Courtney the Clownfish Fairy
978-1-40830-821-9